a min℮dition book

North American edition published 2013 by
Michael Neugebauer Publishing Ltd. Hong Kong

Text copyright © 2012 by Catherine Leblanc
Illustrations copyright © 2012 by Eve Tharlet
English text edited by Martin West
Rights arranged with "minedition" Rights and Licensing AG, Zurich, Switzerland.
Michael Neugebauer Publishing Ltd., Unit 23, 7F, Kowloon Bay Industrial Centre,
15 Wang Hoi Road, Kowloon Bay, Hong Kong. Phone +852 2147 0303,
e-mail: info@minedition.com
This book was printed in July 2013 at L.Rex Printing Co Ltd 3/F., Blue Box Factory
Building, 25 Hing Wo Street, Tin Wan, Aberdeen, Hong Kong, China
Typesetting in Sabon
Library of Congress Cataloging-in-Publication Data available upon request.

ISBN 978-988-8240-51-7

10 9 8 7 6 5 4 3 2 1
First impression

For more information please visit our website: www.minedition.com

Catherine Leblanc

Will You Still Love Me If ...?

Pictures by Eve Tharlet

minedition

Little Bear tears his jacket when he's playing.
Oh dear, Mom will be angry!

Mom is feeling tired. She's been working all day.
"Oh dear, how did you do that? Give it to me and I'll mend it."

Little Bear looks sad.
"What's the matter?" Mom asks, as she looks for the right color thread.
"Mom, I'm sorry I tore my jacket. Do you still love me?"

"Of course I do," Mom says.
"Why wouldn't I love you,
    just because of that?"

As his mom starts to sew with small stitches,
Little Bear rummages through her sewing box.
"If I tore ALL my clothes,
   would you still love me?" he asks.

"If you did that, I'd be very angry," Mom says,
"but I'd still love you!"

Little Bear feels better.

He makes a house out of all the buttons.
Then he asks:
"If I didn't do any work at school and got
a bad report, would you still love me?"

"I'd be very disappointed, but
I would still love you!" says Mom.

"What if I was really naughty and jumped up and down
on my bed and broke it and made a mess in the house?
Would you still love me then?"

"I'd be very upset and I would try to stop you.
But of course I'd still love you!" Mom says.

Then Little Bear asks a silly question.
"What if I was huge and ugly and green
and covered in bugs?"

"Well, that's different," laughs Mom.

But Little Bear keeps going.
"You wait, one day you'll stop loving me!"

"Never!" Mom says. "You'll always be my Little Bear,
and I'll always love you, no matter what.
That will never change!"

But Little Bear wants to be sure.
"And what if I stopped loving you?"

"Then I would be very, very sad and I would cry," Mom says,
"but I wouldn't stop loving you!"

There is something that still worries
Little Bear very much,
but he doesn't dare ask.
Looking down at the floor and fiddling
with his buttons, at last he asks:
"What if you died?"

Mom stops sewing and looks up.
"That's a difficult question to answer.
But I think that even then I would still love you."

"But how would I know?" asks Little Bear.

"Well," Mom says, "when you feel the wind gently stroking
  your fur, see the stream sparkling in the sunlight, and
  when you hear the birds flying above you –
  you will know, deep inside.
  But I'm still here and I'm not dead yet."

Little Bear comes over and cuddles close to his mom.

Then suddenly he leaps down and runs around the room.
He runs around faster and faster, making noises like an airplane.
"Be quiet, Little Bear!" laughs his mom.
Then Little Bear shouts:
"And what if I don't want you to love me any more?"
Mom looks down at her sewing:
"Oh, I would wait until you loved me again.
It wouldn't take very long ..."

Little Bear looks at her round tummy and asks his last question:
"And what if one day you love someone else more than you love me?"

"More than you?" Mom asks. "That's impossible!
I might love someone in a different way.
But it wouldn't change anything because I'll always love YOU!"

She ties a knot, bites off the thread and puts his jacket down.
Little Bear pulls it on. He wants to go out to play with his friends.
Then he asks: "But what if I love somebody else more than I love you?"

Mom looks calmly at Little Bear.
"I will still love you.
You can love whoever you choose."